HANS ALFREDSON   PER ÅHLIN

The Night
the Moon
Came By

Translated by Tiina Nunnally

R&S
BOOKS

Stockholm   New York   London   Adelaide   Toronto

Rabén & Sjögren Stockholm

Translation copyright © 1993 by Rabén & Sjögren
All rights reserved
Originally published in Swedish by Rabén & Sjögren
under the title *När Månen gick förbi*, text copyright © 1991 by Hans Alfredson
Illustrations copyright © 1991 by Per Åhlin
Library of Congress catalog card number: 93-663
Printed in Singapore
First edition, 1993

ISBN 91 29 62246 8

Once upon a time, a long, long time ago, many children believed that trolls existed, as well as elves and ghosts and ghastly creatures with no heads or with five legs. They never came out in the daytime, but at night they would wake up and creep out of their secret hiding places. Emilia didn't believe in such things, but she had a cousin who did. He thought that all those terrifying night creatures really existed …

One gloomy night, a long, long time ago,
the moon came on long legs
past the house where the children lived.

Emilia's cousin woke up when the moon shone on him
through the window. An owl hooted outside. Then he
heard what sounded like heavy footsteps in the attic above
their room!

"Wake up, Emilia!
The Nightlings are jumping around in the
attic," said Emilia's cousin, shaking her.
"What kind of nonsense is that?" said
Emilia.
"I call them Nightlings," said her cousin.
"All those ghastly ghosts and trolls and
gnomes and horrible monsters who might
have twelve eyes on their foreheads and big
claws!

"Can't you hear them sneaking around up there?"
"Ha!" said Emilia. "That's just the cat hunting for mice. Go back to bed."

"Outside, the moon is walking around on its long legs," said her cousin. "So all the Nightlings are on the prowl!

"Can't you hear the creaking and crashing up there?
The River Mare is leaping around, ready to catch
little children and jump into the river with them …

"And the Pallid Count, with his head under his arm, is wandering around with Trax the Magician, who eats nothing but disgusting toads, and Abrafax, the Gruesome Dwarf, who snips off the noses of nitwits with a long pair of tongs!

"And the White Lady, who does nothing but sigh and weep ... and lots of other big and little Nightlings, each one creepier than the last!"

"Let's light a candle and go take
a look upstairs," said Emilia.

And they crept up the creaking stairs to the attic.

"Look over there! A horrible
Nightling with glowing eyes!"
whispered her cousin.
"That's just an old owl," said Emilia.
"He's been living up here in the attic
for years. He helps the cat hunt for
mice."

"Help! What's that over there?"
whimpered her cousin.

"An old wolf skin," said Emilia.
"Ooh! How hideous! It's the
River Mare!"
"That's my old rocking horse," said
Emilia. "And that's the ragged old
Christmas goat made of straw. And the
music box with the wooden thrush on
top, which used to chirp 'Twinkle,
twinkle, little star' when you wound
it up.

"There don't seem to be any of those silly Nightlings up here.
But it would be exciting to see a real ghost with his head under
his arm," said Emilia.
"Don't say things like that," said her cousin. "I really did hear
strange footsteps up here.

"Help! Help! Look over there! Behind the sheet! A Nightling of the worst kind! He's moving!" screamed her cousin, hanging on to Emilia as hard as he could.

He screamed so loud that Aunt Bolster and Sister Twister woke up downstairs and wondered what was going on.

"Who is that screaming up there in the attic?" asked Uncle Tycho, who had been awakened, too. "Let's go up and look."

"What are you children doing up here
in the attic in the middle of the night?"
asked Sister Twister.

"A Nightling!" shrieked Emilia's cousin.
"A horrible, hideous Nightling behind
the curtain over there! He probably
wants to gobble us up!"

"Forgive me. I'm usually allowed to sleep here … But it was so late when I arrived that I didn't want to wake anyone up. I got the ladder and climbed in through the window," said the mysterious little man.

"Ha, ha, ha!" laughed Uncle Tycho.
"It's only the poor vagabond, Lumpenstump.
We always let him sleep up here whenever
he comes this way. You must be hungry.
Here, take my midnight snack and a
glass of milk."
"Thank you, kind sir,"
said Lumpenstump.

"Let's go back to bed now, cousin.
You and your Nightlings!"

And so Emilia and her cousin crawled
back into bed and fell sound asleep ...

"Haven't I told you, Lumpenstump, not to stomp around and wake everyone up when we Nightlings are holding our meeting?" said the Pallid Count.

"Yes, I know," said Lumpenstump. "But it's so cold up here that I have to move around a little."

Cinder the cat didn't want to go to sleep.
He stayed up in the attic and played with the
Nightlings, even though they didn't exist.
Because, as everyone knows, cats don't pay any
attention to whether things exist or not!